Pony Club Princess

Check out Princess Poppy's website
to find out all about the other
books in the series

www.**princesspoppy**.com

Princess Poppy
Pony Club
Princess

written by Janey Louise Jones
Illustrated by Samantha Chaffey

YOUNG CORGI

PONY CLUB PRINCESS
A YOUNG CORGI BOOK 978 0 552 56655 1

Published in Great Britain by Young Corgi,
an imprint of Random House Children's Publishers UK
A Random House Group Company

This edition published 2009

The Random House Group Limited supports The Forest Stewardship
Council (FSC®), the leading international forest certification organisation.
Our books carrying the FSC label are printed on FSC® certified paper. FSC
is the only forest certification scheme endorsed by the leading
environmental organisations, including Greenpeace. Our paper procurement
policy can be found at www.randomhouse.co.uk/environment

MIX
Paper from
responsible sources
FSC® C016897

Young Corgi Books are published by Random House Children's Publishers UK,
61–63 Uxbridge Road, London W5 5SA

www.**princesspoppy**.com
www.**randomhousechildrens**.co.uk

Addresses for companies within The Random House Group Limited
can be found at: www.randomhouse.co.uk/offices.htm

THE RANDOM HOUSE GROUP Limited Reg. No. 954009

A CIP catalogue record for this book is available from the British Library.

Printed and bound by CPI Group (UK) Ltd, Croydon, CR0 4YY

In memory of Jill,
who loved ponies with a passion

Chapter 1

Poppy ambled cheerfully down to Riverside Stables on Barley Farm. She couldn't wait to start riding over jumps on her chestnut pony, Twinkletoes. As she walked into the stable yard, she spotted her cousin Daisy tacking up her pony, Parsley, ready for a canter around the paddock.

"Hi, Poppy," called Daisy.

"Hi," replied Poppy, waving at her cousin.

"Did you get your Pony Club letter about taking part in the competition?" asked Daisy.

"Um, no, not yet. Did you get one?"

"Yes, it's just an 'acceptance to compete' letter, which also explains what will happen at the competition. Look, I've brought it with me," said Daisy.

Poppy peered at the letter Daisy was holding.

The Pony Club Headquarters,
Camomile Cove
From the office of Bluebell Lambton, Senior District
Administrator

Miss Daisy Chain
Shellbay House
Camomile Cove

15th July

Dear Daisy,

We are delighted to tell you that you have been
accepted to compete in the forthcoming Pony Club
regional event. It takes place on Saturday 16th
August at Summer Meadow in Honeypot Hill.
The grounds open at 9.30 am. and early arrival
with horseboxes is highly recommended.

> Rider: Daisy Chain
> Pony Club membership number: 2348 SCZ 12/89
> Pony: Parsley (Full name: "Pocketful of Parsley") –
> Grey Connemara gelding; 8 years old;
> 14 hands high.
> Class: Advanced Jumping Event.
> Number: 1
> Time: First round 12 noon.
> Date: 16th August
> Parking: Horsebox parking ticket enclosed.

We look forward to seeing you at the event,
With best wishes,

Bluebell Lambton

Poppy wished she had her letter too. It all sounded so grown up and exciting.

"Your letter will turn up soon," said Daisy kindly as she folded hers away.

"Yes, I expect so," replied Poppy. "The post hadn't even arrived when I left this morning, so it's probably at home right now. I've applied to join the Pony Club so that I can take part as a member."

"Cool, then we'll both be members," said Daisy with a smile. "Now, come on, we've got to do some practice!"

Down in the paddock, where they had a couple of old practice jumps set up, Daisy gave Poppy lots of tips about jumping.

"Shorten your reins and urge Twinkletoes forward with your legs, Poppy. That way you'll make sure he's under control and he'll be balanced for the jump. Then he'll soar over. It's a bit like flying!"

Poppy listened carefully to what her cousin said and was soon clearing the fences

easily. Daisy was right – as they went over them, Poppy felt as though she and Twinkletoes were flying through the air.

"Wow!" said Daisy. "You're so good! I'll have to make the fences a bit higher this time!"

Poppy beamed with pride and then tried the bigger jumps that Daisy had set up for her. She was concentrating so hard that she completely forgot about her worries over the letter from the Pony Club.

Once she and Twinkletoes were completely exhausted, she watched admiringly as Daisy and Parsley jumped over really high fences. They were so good. Poppy was sure they would win their class in the competition.

When Daisy had finished, Poppy picked up two fallen apples for the ponies as a reward for a hard morning's work. Parsley ate his in a flash while Twinkletoes munched happily on his for ages. Then the two cousins led their ponies back to the stables, chatting about pony accessories.

"Shall we go to Ned's to get the ponies some treats for the competition?" suggested Daisy. "I might get Parsley a new numnah for under his saddle or some new ribbons for his plaits."

Poppy nodded enthusiastically. She loved Ned's, the saddler's shop in Camomile Cove. And it was great to hang out with Daisy as her best friend, Honey, had gone on her annual holiday with her mum and dad. This year they were in Los Angeles in America.

Poppy had missed out on taking part in the last Pony Club competition because she had been so busy preparing for her ballet exam, but she was determined that she

would not miss out on this one. It was the
local Pony Club's first ever competition to
be held in Honeypot Hill. Poppy knew that
all her family and friends would come down
to watch and make a day of it. Her big
ambition was to win a red first-place rosette.
She would fasten it proudly onto Twinkletoes'
bridle and ride around the ring to a standing
ovation from the crowd. She even saw herself
riding at the next
Olympic Games!

Poppy often
got rather carried
away when
she was
daydreaming.
Thinking about
it sensibly, she
realized that, as it
was going to be her
first ever competition,
she would be very lucky

even to be placed in the top three. But more importantly, she needed the letter offering her a place, just like the one Daisy had been sent.

When they got back to Honeysuckle Cottage, Poppy ran through the house and burst into the kitchen.

"Mum! Mum! Has anything arrived in the post from the Pony Club?" she called, hoping that her letter had come.

"From the Pony Club?" asked Mum. "Um, no, there were just a few bills and a postcard from Honey. She says she's having a lovely time, but she misses you."

"Oh!" said Poppy, who would normally have been thrilled to receive a postcard from her best friend. "But Daisy has had a letter confirming her place in the Pony Club competition next month and her letter came this morning so mine should have come too."

Mum looked a bit flustered. She bit her lip anxiously.

"We filled in the application forms together," Poppy reminded her, beginning to feel rather worried, "and you said you'd post them off. Remember?"

"Um, to tell you the truth, darling, I don't remember actually posting those forms at all. Oh dear, I think it might have been on the day when the twins weren't very well a couple of weeks ago – I might have forgotten—"

"But, Mum!" exclaimed Poppy. "It's really important! It's my first ever Pony Club competition!"

"I'm sorry, darling. I just had a lot on my mind . . . Let me have a scout about my desk," said Mum. She soon reappeared with bright red cheeks, holding Poppy's application form, all correctly addressed and with a stamp in place, but just not posted.

The Pony Club
Headquarters,
Camomile Cove,

"Poppy, I'm terribly sorry, I did forget. Don't worry, I'll take this over to the Pony Club offices and explain what's happened," said Mum. "Everything will be fine!"

"The only problem, Aunt Lavender," Daisy told her, "is that all applications were supposed to reach them by last Friday."

Chapter 2

Poppy dissolved into tears, which woke the twins from their nap and they too started crying.

"Oh dear!" said Mum. "What a mess I've got us into. Right, let's sort this out. Can you two girls go and ask Grandpa if he would mind coming over to look after Angel and Archie, and then the three of us can head over to the Pony Club offices and explain my stupid mistake. It'll only take ten minutes, and I'll drop you home afterwards, Daisy."

Poppy dried her eyes, and after a brief

visit to Grandpa's to make the babysitting request, she paced around Honeysuckle Cottage impatiently as her mum got ready.

"I can't eat lunch!" she declared. "I'm far too worried."

But Mum insisted she had a cheese and salad sandwich and soon they were waving goodbye to Grandpa, Angel and Archie.

"I'll take the Camomile Cove road," Mum told them. "I'm sure the turn-off for the Pony Club headquarters is there."

Mum soon turned onto a bumpy country road and they pulled up in the car park

of the regional Pony Club offices. Mum combed her hair and put on some rose-pink lipstick, then headed for the reception area, with Daisy and Poppy following behind.

"Excuse me, and sorry for being a nuisance," Mum said to the lady sitting in reception, "but I have here my daughter's application forms for membership of the Pony Club and for the forthcoming event at Honeypot Hill. I forgot to post them and I wonder if you would consider processing them now, even though they're a few days late?"

Poppy stared at the lady: she looked quite strict, she thought. Her large, confident face was heavily powdered, her lips were stained a dark cyclamen-pink, and her brown wavy hair was set firmly with spray. She wore a navy padded jacket with a silk scarf decorated with riding hats and horses' heads and a badge bearing the name BLUEBELL LAMBTON. Poppy and Daisy recognized it from Daisy's letter.

The lady tutted loudly. "We make the rules for a good reason, you know. We can't be dealing with forms turning up late, right, left and centre. All the places have been offered and we can't change the numbers now, for insurance purposes. I'm afraid you won't be able to compete this time!" she explained.

Poppy couldn't believe what she was hearing. She had been quite sure that Mum would be able to fix everything. It was so unfair, and it was all because of Bluebell Lambton's silly rules. But Poppy was determined to take part. She'd worked so hard for the competition and she wasn't going to miss it. She simply couldn't.

Mum tried to reason with Bluebell.

"I take full responsibility for this. It's not my daughter's fault at all. Is there anything I can do to persuade you to reconsider? You can see how disappointed she is. She has put so much effort into preparing for the competition."

"I'm sorry, but if we bend the rules for one girl, then scores of others will want special treatment too. We look forward to seeing your daughter at the next event."

Bluebell Lambton felt more than a little sorry for the girl, but she had no intention of bending the rules – it was not in her power to do so anyway.

Poppy, Daisy and Mum made their way forlornly out to the car. Mum felt terrible as she looked at Poppy's brave little face, which struggled to hide her disappointment.

Meanwhile Bluebell was deep in thought, wondering if she had been rather harsh, when she heard a phone ringing. Moments later, her colleague, Iris Buxley, appeared from the office behind the reception desk.

"Bluebell," she said, "that was a cancellation for the Novice Jumping Class at the Honeypot Hill competition. The pony is in foal, apparently. So we can fit in another rider. It's number six."

Bluebell looked out of the window and saw the car disappearing into the distance.

"There was a little girl in here just a minute ago, desperate to take part in that

Novice Class," she said. "Her mum had forgotten to post the forms. Do you think we should offer her the place?"

"Definitely!" exclaimed Iris. "We must!"

"But I don't have their details. They had the forms but they seem to have taken them away again. I don't know how I'd get in touch with them," said Bluebell.

"Well, why don't you try and catch them if they've only just left?" said Iris.

"Yes, but neither of us has a car, do we?" said Bluebell, who was starting to think it really would be in the spirit of the Pony Club to offer the place to the little girl who had looked so sad.

"I expect they're heading towards the Camomile Cove road. Why don't you ride? You could cut through the fields to the Periwinkle turn-off and wait for them there, ready to give them the good news! Minty is so nippy she'll get you there in no time."

Bluebell hastily put on her riding hat and gloves. She needed no further encouragement.

Chapter 3

Mum was following the road towards
Periwinkle Lane, desperately trying to cheer
Poppy up. She felt so bad about what had
happened. But Poppy was devastated by the
news that she was not in the competition –
nothing seemed to be working. Even Daisy's
gossip from Smuggler's Cove High, which
Poppy usually loved hearing, couldn't
distract her.

As Mum approached the final turn for
Camomile Cove, she noticed a lady on
horseback waving wildly in the distance.

"Look, Aunt Lavender," said Daisy,

spotting the rider too. "I think she wants us to stop."

Poppy's mum began to slow down and they saw that it was Bluebell Lambton from the Pony Club headquarters. She was flagging them down while also keeping a tight rein on her frisky dark bay mare.

Mum stopped the car and jumped out. Poppy and Daisy rolled down the windows and waved.

"Ah, glad to have caught you!" said Bluebell. "It's about your little girl and the competition . . ."

When Bluebell explained that a place had now become available, Mum was so excited that she hugged the lady's horse, Minty, and then turned back towards the girls. Poppy and Daisy, who had been hanging out of the windows, straining to hear the conversation, had already got out of the car.

Poppy ran up to hug her mum then

turned to Bluebell. "Thank you, Mrs Lambton! Thank you so much!"

Daisy and Poppy then joined hands and danced along the hedgerow, with Daisy making up a celebration song:

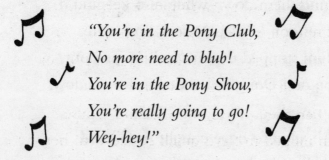

"You're in the Pony Club,
No more need to blub!
You're in the Pony Show,
You're really going to go!
Wey-hey!"

Mum gave Bluebell the envelope with all the forms, which she tucked safely inside her jacket, and they watched as she cantered back towards the Pony Club.

"Yippee, I'm definitely in the competition!" Poppy said as they got back in the car and made their way into Camomile Cove, where the blue sky and even bluer sea met on the horizon. "Thanks for sorting it all out, Mum!"

"All in a day's work, Poppy! I'm just sorry that I forgot to post it in the first place," said Mum, who was feeling hugely relieved.

It was the sort of blunder that would never have happened before she had the twins. She loved them to bits but she sometimes felt sorry for Poppy: it was difficult for her to get used to sharing Mum with her little brother and sister.

When they arrived at Shellbay House, Mum nipped in for a quick coffee with her sister, Delphi, while Poppy and Daisy went off to play in the Summer House.

The next day the cousins met at Riverside Stables again.

"My friend Lily called me last night," said Daisy as the two girls sat in the tack room cleaning the bridles and saddles. "Wait till you hear what she told me!"

Poppy settled down on a bale of straw in the corner of the room with a rosy red apple, eager to hear her cousin's news.

"Apparently Lilac Farrington has enrolled in my event in the pony competition!" revealed Daisy.

"Oh no!" said Poppy, remembering the dreadful problems Lilac had caused for their band, the Beach Babes, at the You're a Star! talent contest. "But she is our friend now, isn't she?"

"Yes, she's always quite sweet to me at Smuggler's Cove High, but you know what she can be like in a competition!" said Daisy.

Poppy nodded. "Does she have a fast pony?"

"He's new. I haven't seen him but I've heard he's called Black Beauty – and lives up to his name!" replied Daisy.

"Wow!" exclaimed Poppy. She thought Lilac's pony sounded gorgeous. "Well, if the competition is going to be tough, we'd better get on with our practice, instead of lazing around here all day!"

"Yeah, you're right," agreed Daisy. "Come on, let's get out into the paddock."

As the girls led their ponies out, Mrs Meadowsweet, the kind farmer's wife, appeared. She was wearing her usual flowery apron and smelled of apple pie. She and her husband owned Riverside Stables.

"Hello, girls!" she called.

"Hello, Mrs Meadowsweet!" the girls replied, making their way towards her.

"Practising for the Pony Club event, dears?"

The cousins nodded.

"You know that our Sally used to compete in shows like this many moons ago?" she began. "Well, we've lots of practice fences and poles in the barn. They haven't seen the light of day for ages! How would you like to set up a course in the paddock – you could time each other and what-not?"

Poppy and Daisy beamed.

"That would be amazing, Mrs Meadowsweet!" said Daisy. "Just show us where they are, and we'll carry them down to the paddock. Thanks so much!"

"They're a bit heavy, love. I'll ask Farmer Meadowsweet to take them along in his trailer. Oh, he used to love it when Sally was eventing. What grand times we had at the competitions! And we loved to watch her practise too."

The girls waited excitedly as the farmer gradually brought over more and more coloured poles, bars, cups, posts and fences.

And with his help, the girls designed and assembled a practice course.

Poppy and Daisy got up onto their ponies and tried it out. Meanwhile, Farmer and Mrs Meadowsweet came out to watch them, bringing with them a picnic of newly baked bread and freshly churned butter.

"Come and get refreshments!" called Mrs Meadowsweet, opening a bottle of her famous oranges and lemons fizz.

Poppy and Daisy were having a
wonderful time. They lay in the sun,
munching on fresh bread, washed down
with the delicious juice, while Mrs
Meadowsweet told them all about Sally's
show-jumping adventures.

Chapter 4

The next morning Poppy and Grandpa travelled over to Camomile Cove for a visit to Ned's. Daisy was waiting for them at the station, as planned.

"Why don't you go to Mum's for coffee, Grandpa?" suggested Daisy. "We'll be about an hour down at the shops."

"Oh, I see," joked Grandpa. "I'm too embarrassing to be seen round town with, am I?"

"In a word, Grandpa, yeah!" laughed Daisy, giving her grandfather a hug.

Poppy loved wandering around the
cobbled streets of Camomile Cove with
her cousin. There were so many pretty shops
selling clothes and shoes, crafts, jewellery
and cakes. The whole town nestled into
the pretty cove so that the golden beach
and blue sea could be seen from almost
every point.

"Are we going for a chocolate nut sundae
at the Lighthouse Café after Ned's?" asked
Poppy. "I've got enough money for both
of us!"

Daisy smiled at her little cousin. "Yes, if

30

we have time. But we must try their new
special. It's a hot-fudge and vanilla–ice-
cream tower with real fudge pieces! It's so
delicious," she told Poppy.

"Yummy!" enthused Poppy as she linked
arms with Daisy.

They made their way along the High
Street, passing Daisy's father's antique shop
and Bijou, their favourite clothes boutique.
Once they reached Ned's they lost
themselves in the smell of saddle soap and
the assortment of gorgeous pony accessories.
There were shelves full of ointments and

31

medicines, vitamins, toothbrushes, hoof picks, pony shampoo, tail guards, fetlock boots in jazzy patterns, blankets, rugs and saddle covers. Poppy loved all the riding hats, jodhpurs, gloves and jackets. The shop had once been an old coaching inn, with stabling for horses while their owners took refreshments inside.

"I can't decide what to buy!" exclaimed Poppy, loving everything she saw.

"Well, what about some pony shampoo so Twinketoes smells of roses at the competition?" suggested Daisy.

"That's a good idea. And what are you going to get for Parsley?" asked Poppy.

"Fetlock boots to protect his legs and fly repellent to keep the pests away!" decided Daisy.

Just as they were paying at the counter, the shop bell jangled and two very glamorous girls came in. They were Lilac Farrington and Fern Zitelli. The two girls were firm friends once more, after their huge falling out over the You're a Star! talent contest.

They were wearing lovely cream jodhpurs, padded green jackets with cord collars, and short brown jodhpur boots, which Poppy thought were very smart.

"Oh, hi, Daisy, hi, Poppy!" called Lilac as she saw the cousins at the cash desk.

"Hello, Lilac," they replied. "Hi, Fern!"

"Are you entering the Pony Club competition?" asked Lilac.

Poppy and Daisy nodded.

"Me too!" said Lilac. "I don't know if you've heard, but I've got a new pony!"

"Oh, someone did mention it," said Daisy. "Are you pleased with him?"

"Just a bit!" Lilac replied. "He's adorable. How would you like to come and see him? He's just along in Sandcastle Stables on the seafront."

Poppy and Daisy looked at each other. This was an offer they simply couldn't refuse. After Lilac and Fern had bought some saddle soap and hoof oil, the four girls strolled along the beach, chatting about ponies and the competition all the way. Poppy thought Lilac seemed much nicer now, even if she was still a bit of a show-off.

Poppy's mouth fell open when she entered Sandcastle Stables. It was a professional stable for racehorses and other liveried

ponies. The yard was pristine, the stall doors
gleamed with varnish and all the horses
looked like they'd been given beauty
treatments. Poppy had never seen anything
like it.

Fern had a pony there called The Duke,
who looked very handsome, and in the stall
next to his was Lilac's new pony.

"And here is Black Beauty!" she
announced proudly as she opened his
stable door.

An exquisitely
beautiful black pony
emerged from the
darkness. At first
Poppy only
saw the white
diamond
between his
eyes; then his
glossy black coat
came into focus.
He had huge

inky-blue eyes, a dainty head and a flowing
black mane and tail. He was the most
perfect pony Poppy had ever seen.

Lilac very kindly asked the girls if they
would like to ride him around the yard.

"No thank you, Lilac," replied Daisy
before Poppy had a chance to say anything.
"I'm afraid we're running out of time.
We said we'd be an hour and we haven't
even been to the Lighthouse Café yet, but

thanks for letting us see him. He's a beauty for sure!"

Poppy was a little disappointed. She would have loved to spend more time with Black Beauty and try him out.

As they walked back to the café, Poppy couldn't stop thinking about Lilac's pony and the amazing stables. Everything there was so much plusher than at Riverside.

"Why don't you keep Parsley here?" asked Poppy. "I'd definitely keep Twinks here if I lived in Camomile Cove."

"Poppy, it's very expensive. All that matters is how much you love your pony and how well you look after him," said Daisy. "And anyway, remember that fabulous practice course we have now at Riverside, with Sally's old jumps!"

"I know," agreed Poppy, "but I would have loved to ride on Black Beauty!"

"Sorry about that," apologized Daisy, "but you should never get on a horse you don't know much about. He's gorgeous, but he looks quite highly strung. We don't want any bumps or bruises before the competition, do we? But at least we've seen him!"

Poppy nodded. She was still daydreaming about Black Beauty as she tucked into her delicious fudge-tower ice cream at the Lighthouse Café. It was nearly as tasty as the chocolate nut sundae, but not quite!

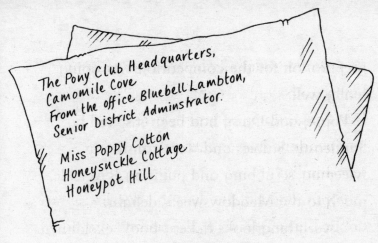

The Pony Club Headquarters,
Camomile Cove
From the office Bluebell Lambton,
Senior District Adminstrator.

Miss Poppy Cotton
Honeysuckle Cottage
Honeypot Hill

Chapter 5

Poppy and Daisy spent the next two and a half weeks working with their ponies, in between other school holiday treats. The highlight for Poppy was when her very own "acceptance to compete" letter from Bluebell Lambton arrived.

She put the letter under her pillow so it wouldn't get lost and she could check it every night. It was official: Poppy was taking part! Luckily, Twinkletoes was jumping perfectly and Parsley was on good form too. The extra jumps and fences the Meadowsweets had put up meant that their

39

preparation for the competition was going really well.

Poppy and Daisy had been inspired by Sandcastle Stables and were constantly sweeping, scrubbing and painting Riverside, much to the Meadowsweets' delight.

"Everything looks tickety-boo!" exclaimed Mrs Meadowsweet one day. "I must get our Sally to come and see it."

A few days before the competition, Poppy was brimming over with excitement. She desperately wanted to win a rosette; she was also dying to see Black Beauty in action. While Daisy took Parsley around the paddock, Poppy decided to try out the shampoo she'd bought for Twinkletoes.

She led him out of his stall and tied him up in the yard. She then found the shampoo and poured it into a black bucket. Next, she turned on the hose and began to add water to the sweet-smelling pony shampoo.

Brilliant, it's really bubbly, she thought.

But as she directed the water into the
bubbles, Poppy began to realize that
something wasn't quite right. The bubbles
began to spill out over the side of the bucket
and onto the yard.

"Oh, no!" she cried, seeing them
multiplying. Surely, if she continued to spray
water over the bubbles, they would soon
disappear, but there were so many soap suds
on the ground that they just formed more
and more bubbles.

Poppy looked around for a drain. She was now soaked through, with bubbles even sitting on the end of her nose. Twinkletoes started trying to sidestep out of the froth – it looked as though he was tap-dancing on a cloud of white bubbles.

"Oh, please go away, bubbles!" said Poppy. "Before Mrs Meadowsweet sees what a mess I've made!"

Just then, Sally, the Meadowsweets' daughter, who ran the Lavender Lake Garden Centre, appeared. She had come to watch the girls practising on her old jumps and to see how well the stables were being run.

"Goodness!" she said. "There are enough bubbles here to bathe all the residents of Honeypot Hill and Camomile Cove!"

"I'm so sorry, Sally. I was just trying to shampoo Twinks and it's all gone a bit too . . . um . . . bubbly!"

"My mum did say it was cleaner than

ever over here," laughed Sally, "and she wasn't wrong! You do realize these bottles of shampoo have enough in them to wash at least twenty ponies?"

"Um, no!" admitted Poppy. "I was so excited about trying it out that I . . . um . . . didn't read the instructions. Sorry."

"Not to worry, it's not a disaster," said Sally. "I think the best thing to do is wash all the ponies at Riverside with these soap suds. It's better than wasting them all. Come on, Poppy. Let's tie them up out here and give them all a good shampooing!"

They led the other ponies into the yard. There was a gorgeous palomino pony called Nilla and a bay mare called Plum as well as several little Shetland ponies and an adorable dappled grey called Fred. Even Patch the stable dog got involved, darting around between the ponies and snapping at the bubbles.

Poppy and Sally had so much fun hosing and sponging that they didn't notice Twinkletoes shivering as he stood in the cold water.

"What's all this?" asked Daisy, surprised by the scene that met her when she returned from the practice paddock.

"There's been a bit of an accident," explained Poppy, her nose and hair still covered in soap suds. She told her cousin all about what she had done.

"Want us to give Parsley a bath? There are still loads of bubbles floating around!"

Daisy nodded and laughed. "Thanks, Poppy. That would be brilliant."

Chapter 6

The next morning, Poppy ate a good
breakfast of porridge oats made with
creamy milk and sweetened with a dash of
honey, followed by a warm butter croissant
topped with Granny Bumble's strawberry
jam. With only three days to go before the
event, she was trying to remember
everything Daisy had taught her. She
vaguely heard the phone ringing.

"It's David Sage on the line for you,
Poppy!" called Mum. "It's about Twinkletoes
– he's not well."

"Oh, no!" cried Poppy as she dashed

into the hall to pick up the phone.

When she finished talking to David, she looked very worried indeed.

"What is it, darling?" asked Mum, concerned.

"David thinks Twinks has caught a chill," explained Poppy, not even thinking about the competition, just worried about her beloved pony. "Can I go down to the stables now?"

"Yes, sweetheart." Mum smiled at her. "I'm sure he'll be fine. David will know how to make him better and Twinkletoes is a strong little thing."

When Poppy arrived at the stables, Mrs Meadowsweet came out to meet her. She looked very anxious, which made Poppy feel even more worried.

"Oh, Poppy! Bad news, I'm afraid. Twinkletoes developed a chill and then a high temperature during the night. David has checked him over and says he'll be back before lunch to look at him again. In the meantime, we've got to keep him warm and get him to drink as much water as possible."

Poppy burst into tears. "It's all my fault for getting him soaked yesterday!" she wailed.

"Don't be silly, Poppy. Sally told me all about that, but none of the other ponies are ill and they were all wet too, weren't they? It's just one of those things, dear. David suggested that you should rest Twinkletoes for a couple of days – then he should be fine. Oh, look, here comes Daisy!"

Daisy was very sorry to learn that
Twinkletoes was unwell and did her best to
comfort Poppy. The girls decided to go and
see for themselves how the pony was doing.
They found him lying down in his stall with
his head hanging low, looking very sorry for
himself. He nickered softly when he saw
Poppy, trying to show that he was pleased to
see her. She dived in beside him and hugged
him tight.

"I've helped to make you better before
and I'll do it again!" she promised. "Daisy,

would you sit with
him just while I go
home? I need to get
some things."

Daisy agreed and
Poppy dashed home
as fast as her legs would
take her. As quick as
a flash, she packed an
overnight bag with
pyjamas, toothbrush,
change of clothes and,
most important of all,
her flower healing
wand, which had
worked so well when
Grandpa was sick.

"Mum!" she called.
"See you tomorrow.
I'm going to sleep at the
stables until Twinkletoes
is better!"

Mum saw Poppy disappear down the path like a streak of lightning. She put the twins in the pram, gathered together some fruit, bread, cheese and bottled water on the pram basket for lunch, and followed Poppy down to the stables. Mum loved Twinkletoes too, but there was no way she was going to let Poppy sleep there.

When Mum arrived, she found Poppy offering Twinkletoes a baby's bottle full of water. Daisy had supported Poppy all she could, but now she had to catch the train home to meet her friends, Lily and Rose.

Mum and Poppy stayed with Twinkletoes all morning while the twins played with the

chickens and kittens. At lunch time they
heard David Sage come into the yard.
He examined the little chestnut pony
thoroughly. Poppy was desperately hoping
that he would say that Twinkletoes was well
on the way to recovery, but it was bad news.

"I'm afraid it's gone to his chest," David
told them. "It's more serious than I thought.
We do know he's a little fighter but he's
going to need lots of looking after."

He left a bottle of medicine to be given
to Twinkletoes.

"Poppy," said Mum after they'd given the
pony some medicine and made sure he was
as comfortable as possible, "you really should

come home now – we can come back in time for his next dose."

But Poppy shook her head with such determination that Mum knew there was no point in trying to persuade her headstrong daughter to change her mind.

"OK, then. If you really do insist on staying here all day and all night, I'll send Dad down with two sleeping bags as soon as he gets home from work. I'm sure Twinks will be fine, Poppy, especially with you looking after him. Try not to worry too much," she said. "I'll let Mrs Meadowsweet know what the plan is."

When Mum and the twins had left, Poppy burst into tears. She was so worried about her pony and was quite sure it was all her fault, whatever everyone else said.

Mrs Meadowsweet came down to keep Poppy company for the rest of the afternoon. When Dad arrived in the early evening, she went back up to the farmhouse.

Dad and Poppy laid out their beds in the stall, checked that Twinkletoes was comfortable, and then, at Mrs Meadowsweet's invitation, went up to the farmhouse for some supper.

When they got back, Dad tucked Poppy up in her sleeping bag with a fluffy pillow from the farmhouse under her head and settled down beside her. Poppy immediately fell into a deep and exhausted sleep.

David Sage dropped by for a last look at the sick pony, but he couldn't see much improvement.

"She's devoted, that's for sure!" he said to Dad as they both looked at Poppy, lying asleep in the straw. "I'll go over to the big veterinary practice in Camomile Cove first thing tomorrow – they might have some stronger antibiotics. I'll see you then."

"Thanks, David," said Dad. "I appreciate all your help."

"Yeah, well, it's my job. But this little pony, he's a bit special," said David. "And so is this little princess."

Poppy woke very early the next morning and felt all achy. Dad was still fast asleep. Poppy looked over at her pony. He seemed far worse. He looked at her with big, sad eyes, as if to say, "What's going on? What's wrong with me?"

Poppy sat by his side until David arrived with the antibiotics. After he'd had given

Twinkletoes his jab he turned to Poppy.

"I hear you are due to compete in a pony competition on Twinks soon?"

"Yes, in two days' time. We've been practising for ages," said Poppy.

"Well, Twinkletoes is definitely going to get better but I'm afraid I don't think he'll be well enough in time for that," said David. "I'm sorry. Maybe you could use one of the Meadowsweets' ponies. I'm sure they'd let you ride Plum, for instance."

Poppy thought about this for a moment. "I only really want to ride on Twinkletoes," she said, "but I suppose I could think about trying out another a pony. But only if I see that Twinkletoes is getting better – otherwise I'd never be able to concentrate."

Poppy's dad was now wide awake and he liked David's idea about Poppy riding another pony. He decided to find out if this might be possible and headed back to Honeysuckle Cottage to ring the Pony Club.

Meanwhile Poppy lovingly plaited Twinkletoes' mane and tail and softly brushed his coat. She gave him drinks of water, while Mrs Meadowsweet kept an eye on things and brought Poppy a delicious bowl of creamy porridge, drizzled with raspberry jam.

Dad soon got through to Bluebell Lambton. He explained the situation with Poppy's pony and told her that another

pony was available
at the stables.

"I'm sorry, Mr
Cotton, but the rules
state that only the
registered pony can
compete.

So, unless
Twinkletoes gets
better, Poppy will
not be able to take
part," Bluebell told
him. Again, she felt
very sorry, but she
had done as much

as she could for Poppy Cotton; this was one
thing she couldn't alter.

Dad thanked her and said goodbye. He
was disappointed that this solution wasn't
going to work and nervous about telling the
news to Poppy. She would be so upset if she
couldn't compete. It was bad enough that

her beloved pony was ill, but this would be
too much.

"I'll go down to Riverside to tell
her, James," said Mum. "You look after
the twins."

Chapter 7

When Mum reached Twinkletoes' stable, she couldn't believe her eyes. The plucky little pony was standing up and Poppy was gently leading him round with Mrs Meadowsweet looking on.

"It's amazing, Mum!" exclaimed Poppy. "Ever since David brought him that other medicine, he's been getting a bit better every hour."

"It's true, Lavender," agreed Mrs Meadowsweet. "I've never seen anything quite like it! I'm sure Poppy's healing flower wand has helped too!"

Poppy didn't want to relax just yet, but she felt sure that the signs were good. Just then, David Sage arrived.

"Wow, he's up!" he said, surprised but delighted at this development. "I'll give him another shot and we'll see how he is mid-afternoon. You're doing a great job, Poppy! I've never seen a recovery like it. It's practically a miracle!"

Poppy cuddled Twinkletoes and willed him to get even stronger. Now that he was out of serious danger at last, she desperately wanted him to be well enough for the competition the next day. She was sure he would recover in time, and when Mum told her that, according to Pony Club rules, she could only compete on Twinkletoes, Poppy became even more determined that he should recover.

Daisy came to help out and Poppy went home for a lovely bubble bath, feeling so

much better about her pony, but quickly
made her way back to the stables.

That evening, David came to check on
Twinkletoes and to give him another dose
of medicine. He was quietly confident that
the brave little pony would be well enough
to compete, but he didn't want to get Poppy's
hopes up just in case he had a relapse.

He told Poppy that Twinkletoes was
well enough for a gentle ride around the
practice paddock. She tried him out and
was absolutely delighted when he jumped
perfectly.

Poppy went back to Honeysuckle Cottage
that night and had a lovely deep sleep on

her fluffy princess bed, keeping her fingers crossed that everything would be OK.

The next morning was the BIG day! Poppy had been so busy looking after Twinkletoes that she had hardly had a chance to think about it. She dressed carefully in pale-cream jodhpurs, a velvet-collared navy-blue jacket and riding boots. She pinned a red poppy from the garden onto the lapel of her jacket for luck and headed down to Riverside Stables to meet Daisy.

When she arrived at the stables, she quickly checked on her pony, who was looking eagerly out of his stall, then raced over to Mrs Meadowsweet to find out whether there was any news from David.

"Has David been today?" she asked breathlessly, without even pausing to say hello to the farmer's wife.

"Yes, Poppy," smiled Mrs Meadowsweet. "He's already examined Twinks."

"Well, what did he say?" asked Poppy impatiently. "Can we compete in the show?"

"If you'd just let me get a word in, Poppy, I'll tell you what he said!" laughed Mrs Meadowsweet.

Chapter 8

The kindly farmer's wife explained to Poppy that David had left a message with Farmer Meadowsweet early that morning to say that Twinkletoes was officially well enough to compete. His temperature was normal and the antibiotics had cleared up the chest infection.

"But David will be at the competition to keep an eye on him!" added Mrs Meadowsweet. "And so will I! Goodness, what a lot of dramas we've had round here of late!"

Poppy was so delighted that she hugged

Mrs Meadowsweet and dashed off to
give Twinkletoes a treat for being such a
brave pony.

Dad drove the horsebox with Parsley and
Twinkletoes on board down to Summer
Meadow, at the edge of Honeypot Hill, near
Wildspice Woods. Poppy and Daisy sat in
the back with their ponies. They were very
quiet and thoughtful.

When they arrived, Poppy was amazed to
see what a big event it was. There were rows
of horseboxes and hundreds of gorgeous
ponies parading around the paddock. She
noticed all kinds of fabulous pony gear and
all the girls and grooms were wearing
amazing riding clothes. There was a balloon
stall, ice-cream sellers, as well as hot-snack
vans and a proper little outdoor café called
The Horseshoe. It reminded Poppy of the
annual Fair Day, only everything was
horse-themed. Little stalls were selling hats
and boots, silk scarves, tie-pins, cosy sweaters

and grooming kits. Poppy adored all the horsy bits and pieces.

The main focus was on the two show rings filled with different-coloured jumps, where the contests between the young Pony Club members would soon take place.

Dad found a nice sunny spot for the horsebox and the girls led the ponies out and started to tack them up.

"Mum, Grandpa and the twins will be here soon and Granny Bumble is bringing a picnic basket. And, Daisy, I think your family will be over by mid-morning too, is that right?" asked Dad.

"Yes, Uncle James. They always turn up to cheer me on!" she replied.

Just then Poppy's eye was caught by an elegant pony in the practice paddock. It was Black Beauty! Daisy looked a little concerned – he was jumping quite magnificently and he and Lilac looked wonderful. This was certainly going to

be a tough competition for her.

Before long Poppy's whole family and her school friends turned up to support her. They had all heard how ill Twinkletoes had been and were very pleased that he had got better in time. Poppy was delighted to see everyone at Summer Meadow but she was still a little concerned about how her brave little pony would cope, having been so sick just the day before.

Soon it was time for the Novice Jumping Class. This was Poppy's category – and who

should be ringing the bell at the start of the
course but Bluebell Lambton! After five
patchy rounds from girls of around Poppy's
age, it was her turn.

"Number six to the entrance of the ring,"
called a steward.

Poppy and Twinkletoes trotted in proudly.
Bluebell smiled encouragingly at her,
pleased to see that she had made it to the
competition after all. Poppy knew she had
to focus on achieving a clear round and not
let anything else distract her.

She was aware of her family cheering her on as the bell rang and her time in the ring officially began. But as soon as she was on her way, Poppy could hear nothing but the sound of Twinkletoes' hooves on the grass and her own heart beating: she just concentrated on following the course.

There were so many ways she could lose precious points: for knocking a fence down or for taking too long, or even for going round the fences in the wrong order. Daisy had told her to go as fast as she could so as

not to get time faults, but then confused her
by saying that it was important to take her
time so she didn't knock any fences down.

Poppy could only do her best.

Chapter 9

"Come on, Twinks, you can do it, boy!" she whispered as they cantered towards the first fence, which was a low wall. Pop! They made it over. But Poppy knew that she had to rein her pony in before the second. If he wasn't under control, he would never be able to clear it. She held him steady and, with another bunny-hop, he was over. She turned him round to the left to go over the stile. Clear! Hooves and heart were pounding. Now on to the triple jump . . . She usually knocked one of these down. Over the first, over the second and over the third, but at the third element – clatter – the poles came down. Twinkletoes had just snicked it with his hind leg!

But she mustn't let it bother her – Poppy knew they were going quite fast and still had a chance, even with one fence down, so long as their time was good and they had no other faults. Before she knew it they were cantering towards the final fence, the water feature . . .

"Come on, Twinks, you can fly!" she encouraged the plucky little chestnut pony.

He put his heart and soul into it. Poppy knew instinctively that he had taken off nicely. He seemed to soar through the air as if he had wings and he cleared the water easily – she was hardly splashed at all. Poppy leaned forward to hug him from the saddle. She was so proud of her darling little pony. He might not be the most stylish jumper but he tried so very hard.

Twinkletoes gave a little celebratory

bunny-hop at the end, which delighted the crowd but almost sent Poppy flying! Now that her round was over, she started to hear sounds around her again.

"Miss Poppy Cotton leaves the ring with just four faults and an excellent time of sixty-six point seven seconds," announced the commentator. "Well done, Poppy! And now please welcome Matilda Yarrow and Flashdance into the ring!"

There were still several more riders to go in Poppy's class. Everyone was keen to congratulate her as she made her way out of the ring. Mum and Dad were thrilled. Daisy was incredibly proud of her little cousin's achievement in her first ever jumping competition. Even Poppy's cousin Edward applauded her.

"It's all down to Twinkletoes!" said Poppy modestly, before adding, "Well, I suppose I was pretty amazing too!"

Everyone laughed and Poppy jumped down off Twinkletoes and gave him a kiss and a huge juicy carrot. David checked him over and pronounced him in good shape.

"All thanks to Princess Poppy's healing wand!" he said, smiling. "I might need to borrow that occasionally, Poppy!"

Poppy tied up her pony by the horsebox and changed her riding boots for comfortable shoes. Meanwhile Lilac and Daisy took their ponies into the practice ring: their class was starting in the main ring after the novice competition was over.

Poppy and Edward decided to lay out the picnic rug and watch the other novices. Edward, even though he often bugged

Poppy, was a very useful companion: he had sat through hundreds of these events in the past, watching Daisy and her friends, and he knew all about the ponies and riders.

Matilda Yarrow had a good round, with only one fence down, but was rather slow at 75 seconds, and then the steward called for the next competitor.

Poppy really hoped that she would stay in first place. That red rosette was in her sights now, and before long she was daydreaming again . . .

She imagined what the commentator might say about her as she stood in the ring, waiting to be awarded first prize:

"The first prize goes to the most talented rider of her generation, Princess Poppy Cotton, on Lord Twinkletoes. They have battled against adversity. They have stood up to a ballet teacher who hates riding, a forgetful mother who failed to post the application form for the competition, strict

Pony Club rules, not to mention a high
temperature and a chest infection in
Twinkletoes brought on by tap-dancing in
soap suds. And here they are today, breaking
a world record, making history in their own
back yard . . ."

Chapter 10

"Cucumber sandwich, Poppy dear?" said Granny Bumble, who was sitting on the rug with Poppy and Edward.

"Oh, um, yes, please. I was miles away," said a startled Poppy. "I should be paying attention to how all the other riders in my class are doing. Oops!"

Poppy and Edward chatted as they kept score. Poppy was delighted – it seemed she was in with a real chance. There were no clear rounds, and everyone else was slower: her position was strong.

The final rider was Pollyanna Willoughby.

"I don't think you've got much to worry about, Poppy," said Edward. "I saw Pollyanna at Daisy's last show: her pony is a bit chubby and very slow!"

Poppy smiled. It seemed the red rosette would soon be hers. But Edward had not bargained on Pollyanna Willoughby's new grey pony with a white blaze on his face. He was called Lightning and he looked very fast and strong. Poppy realized that she might be knocked off the top slot after all.

She and Edward stood up and watched intently as the bell sounded and Pollyanna began her round. Lightning was well named. He took off at breakneck speed and jumped

beautifully. Poppy felt sure she was going
to lose out to this pair. As they approached
the water jump, she knew they were much
faster than she had been.

That's what I get for daydreaming that
I've already won! Poppy scolded herself.

Lightning cantered up to the jump. Poppy
could hardly bear to watch. She'd come so
close to winning – she would be devastated
if she was beaten by the final competitor.

As Lightning soared over the jump, he
seemed to glance down at the stretch of
water beneath him. He twisted in mid-air
and then his hind legs came down and
splashed right in the middle of the water
feature! Pollyanna struggled to bring him
under control, but he didn't like the water
one little bit! Eventually he emerged, shook
himself and carried on, but they now had
four faults, just like Poppy and Twinkletoes,
and surely they'd lost a lot of time at that
last jump.

Poppy and Edward couldn't quite work out if it was a better round overall than Poppy's or not. As they were trying to hear what the commentator had to say, they were distracted by the Advanced Class starting to assemble.

"I think he said the winner of the Novice Class would be announced at the prize-giving at four o'clock, but I didn't hear Pollyanna's final score!" said Granny Bumble, who had been trying to listen.

Poppy could hardly bear the suspense – she was desperate to know whether she had won or not, but there was nothing she could do about it now. She had to support Daisy, so she and Edward dashed over to the main ring.

Parsley and Daisy were going first. Parsley looked fit and sleek and performed beautifully, even though it was a very tricky course. He had no faults and a time of 65 seconds. After some other good performances

– though none as fast as Daisy's – Lilac, the
last competitor, came in on the gorgeous
Black Beauty.

They made a lovely team and also had
a clear round. No one could believe it when
the commentator announced their time:
also 65 seconds! It was a tie between Daisy
and Lilac!

The judges announced that at three
o'clock there would be a jump-off on a
shortened course between Daisy on Parsley

and Lilac on Black Beauty. Luckily Lilac
was being a good sport on this occasion,
but Daisy was very nervous. She had
been working with Parsley for years,
whereas Lilac had only just bought Black
Beauty. It really mattered to Daisy that
she won.

When the new course was ready, Daisy
decided to walk it first; she asked Poppy to
keep an eye on Parsley for her.

"OK, Daisy, no problem," said Poppy.
"I'm watching Twinkletoes anyway."

Poppy checked that Parsley was securely
tied to the horsebox, next to his best friend,
Twinkletoes, and settled down on the picnic
rug with a pony magazine. Just then Edward
returned from a blacksmith's demonstration
of how to shoe a pony. He was full of news
about the showground.

"Want to go for a wander round the
stalls?" he asked Poppy. "We could get an ice
cream. There's loads of fun stuff going on!"

"I'd love to, but I'm meant to be looking after the ponies," replied Poppy as she looked around to see whether anyone else might be able to keep an eye on Parsley and Twinkletoes for her.

Unfortunately, all her friends and family seemed to be off doing other things – there was no one around to look after the ponies. She felt she was missing out on all the fun.

"They're both tied up and we won't be long," said Edward persuasively.

As the hot sun beat down on her, Poppy thought an ice cream sounded lovely, and she really wanted to have a look at the stalls.

"Oh, come on then, let's be quick," she replied, "but don't tell Daisy."

Poppy and Edward strolled around looking at stalls and enjoying toffee-ripple ice-cream cornets, but before long Poppy began to feel bad about breaking her promise to Daisy.

"I think I'd better go back and check on Parsley and Twinks. Daisy will be back soon," she said.

"OK then," agreed Edward. "Let's go."

When they arrived at the horsebox, Twinkletoes was happily munching on some juicy-looking grass, but Parsley was nowhere to be seen! Poppy's mouth went dry with fear.

"Oh, my goodness! Parsley has totally vanished!" she screamed.

"Maybe Daisy came back for him while we were away? Ponies don't just vanish," said Edward, who was also worried – after all, he had persuaded Poppy to leave the ponies alone in the first place.

At that moment they both spotted Daisy, on her way back from the ring. How was Poppy going to tell her that she had failed to look after her pony?

Chapter 11

"Oh, Daisy, come quickly!" sobbed
Poppy, waving frantically at her cousin.
"I don't know what to do. Parsley has
disappeared!"

"What?" said Daisy, running as fast as she
could towards the horsebox. "How can he
be missing? I've only been away for fifteen
minutes and you've been looking after him,
haven't you? If this is a joke, then it's not
very funny when I have such an important
jump-off ahead of me."

Poppy hung her head in shame. "It's not
a joke. I wish it was. I'm so sorry, I left him

alone for a few minutes. We went for a wander and an ice cream, that's all."

Daisy was very cross and upset that her cousin had broken her promise.

"I bet Edward is behind this! And to think you left Twinks as well, after all he's been through," she said.

Word of Parsley's mystery disappearance spread like wildfire through Summer Meadow. The jump–off, which all the crowds were so looking forward to, could not take place until he was found. It seemed as if Poppy's carelessness had ruined the whole show: everything had come to a complete standstill. The commentator made an announcement on the loudspeaker.

"Attention please. This is an important announcement. A grey pony almost fourteen hands in height, answering to the name of Parsley, has vanished from the meadow. Can everyone please stop what they are doing and join in the search for him? Look in your horseboxes and behind stalls. Please report any sightings to the administration team. The Advanced Class jump-off cannot proceed until this pony is found. Thank you!"

Poppy felt sick. It was all her fault. Daisy had every right to be angry with her. But this made her all the more determined to fix everything.

Poppy's mum and dad, and Daisy's too, were working out a plan. They decided to split up into pairs to look for Parsley, while Edward stayed with Twinkletoes.

But there was no sign of the pony. It was as if he had never existed. Everyone was hunting high and low, all to no avail. At one point someone triumphantly showed Daisy a grey pony, but a girl came after him shouting, "Hey! That's Angus. He's mine!"

Poppy and Mum went round every
horsebox, asking people very politely to
check for Parsley. Poppy's face was smeared
with tears and dust.

"What does he like best of all, Poppy?"
asked Mum. "That might give us a clue
to where he might have headed. Just
think, darling."

Poppy concentrated very hard on Mum's
question. "Well, he does love apples!" she
replied, remembering how Parsley always
guzzled them at top speed.

Mum looked as if she'd had an idea. "Poppy, come with me. Let's check out the orchard in Wildspice Woods. He might just have followed the smell of ripe summer apples in the air!"

Poppy thought this was unlikely, but she felt so desperate that she was prepared to give anything a try. As they entered the dense woods, she felt as though they were looking for a needle in a haystack.

"We'll never find him in here! It's so dark," she moaned, looking up at the canopy of leaves that shaded the sunlight overhead.

Mum was gazing at the ground. The soft grassy pathway was indented with hoof

marks – she was sure they were going to find him. "Not far to the orchard now!" she cheerfully.

Poppy was exhausted and thirsty. The last thing on her mind was her own success in the Novice Class – all that mattered was her cousin's pony.

"I hope he's here – if he's gone the other way, onto a road, it could be so dangerous!" she said.

Mum led Poppy into the orchard. "Delphi and I always used to come here to gather apples for your granny's delicious pies and crumbles!" she told her. "Come this way – these are pear trees; the apple trees are further on!"

As they walked into the sweet-smelling avenue of green apple trees, they heard a rustle, then a loud crunching noise.

"Shhh!" said Mum. "Be very quiet . . ."

She pulled back the branches of one especially laden tree, and there was Parsley! He was gorging on the wonderful apples as if he hadn't a care in  the world. Poppy laughed with relief and tried to hug the naughty pony, but he made off in the opposite direction. Perhaps he sensed that his private apple-munching party had come to an end.

"Come here, Parsley, there's a good boy!" said Poppy.

"Get a few apples and we'll coax him

back to Summer Meadow!" suggested Mum,
feeling so relieved that she started to giggle
and couldn't stop.

"Good idea," replied
Poppy as she picked some
lovely juicy apples and
showed them to Parsley.

Finally, between them,
Mum and Poppy lured Parsley back to the
show. When someone saw them coming
through the gates, word soon spread back to
Daisy, who ran across to greet them. Poppy
explained where they had found the pony
and how mischievous he had been and
apologized again for leaving him alone.

"Don't worry, Poppy-kins – it could have
happened on anyone's watch!" said Daisy,
delighted to have her pony back. "At least
you found him again!"

"All thanks to Mum!" said Poppy.

Daisy stroked Parsley's nose and gave him
a kiss. "You and apples!" she scolded him

gently on hearing that he had been binging in the orchard. "I'll get you a whole barrel of apples if you behave for the rest of the day!"

Without further ado, the competition organizers announced that the drama was over: Daisy and Parsley would soon be in the ring for the jump-off.

Lilac was relieved to hear that Parsley was safe and well. She would have been very disappointed if the jump-off had been cancelled. Her mum, dad and grandfather, Colonel Forster, were all proudly supporting her. This was Black Beauty's first show and she was excited at the prospect of winning. But she had to win fair and square – no more cheating.

Daisy was first into the ring. She and Parsley looked unbeatable as they cantered round. But just before the starting bell sounded, Parsley froze, rolling his eyes, and then shied.

Poppy followed his gaze and realized that
he had spotted something rustling in the
nearby bushes. She soon realized that it was
two balloons stuck in the bush, bobbing
together. Daisy hadn't seen it, but she knew
that something was wrong from the way
Parsley's body had tensed. She tried to
soothe him, but he began to tremble. Then,

as her pony gave a huge buck, Daisy was thrown into the air and ended up lying on the ground, quite motionless.

Chapter 12

The event First Aider rushed to her side, closely followed by Poppy and the rest of the family. Daisy's eyes were shut tight and her breathing was ragged.

"Daisy, wake up!" wailed Poppy. "I couldn't have done this without you! Now you need to win your event. I know you can do it. Please wake up, Daisy! You've got to win!"

The First Aider checked Daisy over, examining her very thoroughly, especially for neck and back injuries. As she did so, Daisy opened her eyes and smiled. After

another few moments she was helped to
her feet. Soon she looked quite normal and
the colour slowly came back into her
cheeks. Lilac came over to see how her rival
was doing.

"Let's cancel the jump-off – we'll call it a
draw," she suggested. "Your health comes
first, Daisy, and that was quite a fall."

"Yes, you must take care, darling," said
Aunt Delphi. "You don't have to do this, you
know. We think you're the best already!"

Daisy smiled, but she was determined to
mount up again. "I don't really care about

anything except Parsley, but the best thing
after a spook is to carry right on, otherwise
we'll both go on being nervous," she said
bravely.

Fortunately, after she's rested for ten
minutes, the First Aider declared her fit
to ride.

Everyone was full of admiration as she
pluckily gathered herself together.

"Good luck!" Poppy called as her cousin
remounted Parsley. "You're the best!"

Daisy smiled back at Poppy. She wanted
to perform well for her little cousin, who

had ridden so amazingly and had listened to every word of advice, even if she didn't always keep her promises!

Daisy cantered round the ring to loud cheers. She motioned to everyone to keep the noise down. "Sshh! We don't want to scare the pony!" she called.

"Well," said the commentator some moments later, "I'm sure you were all thinking that this jump-off was never going ahead, but we have been assured that Daisy and Parsley are quite well enough to take part. So, you're off at the bell, Daisy. Here we go!"

The bell rang, Daisy spoke softly to Parsley and off they went at a nice steady pace. Parsley had never jumped so well, clearing each fence with room to spare. As he approached the final fence, everyone held their breath. Daisy kept him steady and leaned forward in the saddle, helping him as much as she could. He flew across it, neatly

tucking in his hind legs. It was a perfect round with an excellent time of 42 seconds.

Now it was Lilac's turn. She entered the ring looking beautifully poised on her perfect pony. His coat shone inky-black in the sunlight, his hooves gleaming and his mane and tail neatly groomed. And Lilac was equally immaculate: she wore a black riding jacket with a velvet collar, and a black velvet hat. Her jodhpurs were almost pure white and her leather boots looked hand-made. They made an impressive sight. But although Poppy was impressed, she thought they seemed almost too perfect, for show rather than a fun-loving and devoted team.

As the bell rang, they set off steadily, popping over the fences nicely, when suddenly, the balloons that had so alarmed Parsley, freed themselves from the bush and started drifting towards the course. Black Beauty froze like a statue in the middle of

the ring. Lilac didn't know her new pony
well and was terrified that he might buck
and rear. She held on for dear life as time
seemed to stand still while Black Beauty
decided what to do.

Poppy watched open-mouthed: she didn't
want Lilac to be thrown, but she also
desperately wanted Daisy to beat the girl
who had caused them so much heartache in
the past. Eventually the wind blew the
balloons away and out of Black Beauty's
view. The pony settled down again and

carried on to the next fence. But he was less steady and focused, looking for the balloons out of the corner of his eye. He clipped the last two fences with his heels and ended up with eight faults.

It was all over at last. Daisy had won the jump-off fair and square, and everyone agreed she deserved first prize. It had been so exciting.

Lilac jumped down from Black Beauty and ran over to congratulate Daisy, who dismounted and offered her congratulations to Lilac as well.

With all the excitement of the last two hours, Poppy realized that she still didn't know if she had won her competition or not.

She began to tidy herself up, putting her riding boots back on, then brushing her hair and replacing her riding hat. The commentator announced that all competitors should meet in the main ring for the grand prize-giving.

All of Poppy and Daisy's family and friends stood at the ringside to watch the ceremony. Poppy was surprised to see that the lady handing out the rosettes and silver cups was dear Mrs Meadowsweet. She was wearing a lovely big straw hat and a pretty summer tea dress in pansy colours of pink, yellow and purple.

It turned out that Poppy had narrowly beaten Pollyanna. They both had four faults, but Poppy's time was quite a bit faster. She was named as the winner of the Novice Class. Poppy was ecstatic. A red rosette after all! And presented by Mrs Meadowsweet – what could be more perfect?

Poppy stood proudly on the boxes in

the middle of the ring for the prize-giving. She and her cousin Daisy couldn't believe that after all the disasters, bad luck and dramas they'd encountered, they were each sporting a red first-place rosette.

"Daisy, you are the official Pony Club Princess, because you taught me everything I know!" said Poppy, smiling.

Daisy beamed. She wasn't too old to be a princess. And being a Pony Club Princess was just perfect.

Turn over to read an extract from the next Princess Poppy book,
Fairytale Princess . . .

Chapter One

Poppy thought that her teacher, Miss Mallow, was absolutely brilliant. She was so kind and she was always thinking up ways to make her lessons really interesting and fun. Poppy especially loved Monday mornings because every week they had what Miss Mallow called "circle time". This was when each and every one of the children was given an opportunity to share something that was special to them with the rest of the class. It was called "circle time" because Miss Mallow made them put their chairs in a big circle in the middle of the classroom so that they could all see everything that was being shown.

Poppy nearly always brought in something.

One Monday, she was especially pleased with what she had brought – it was one of her most treasured possessions and she couldn't wait to show it. When Miss Mallow announced that it was circle time, everyone moved their chairs into position and then she went round the class asking each child if they had anything to share. By the time she came to Poppy, Poppy was almost bursting with excitement! She reached into her school bag, pulled out her special item and held it up for everyone to see.

"I got this from my grandpa. It's a book of fairytales and Grandpa told me that it is over a hundred years old! It belonged to Grandpa's granny, who was my great-great-granny Mellow!"

"That is lovely!" exclaimed Miss Mallow. "A true piece of history. In fact, it might be useful today. You see, I have something to share with all of you too."

"Maybe she's getting married to Prince Charming!" whispered Poppy to her best friend, Honey. But that was not Miss Mallow's news.

"Children, as you know, builders are working on the school hall at the moment and it is due to be ready in eight weeks," began Miss Mallow. "The stage will be redesigned with new lighting and scenery, there will be new flooring, the roof is being fixed so there will be no more leaks, and we'll have some lovely new chairs and curtains. The Headmistress has invited a special guest to reopen the hall. However, I think we should do something to make the reopening even more special so I've decided that we will put on our very own musical show! What do you think?"

"Yeah!" chorused the whole class.

"Yes, Poppy, what is it?" asked Miss Mallow, noticing that Poppy's hand had gone up as soon as she'd told everyone about her plan.

"Um, who is the special guest? And which show are we going to do?"

"Well, I was actually just coming to both things," smiled Miss Mallow, thinking how impatient and inquisitive Poppy was. "The guest is Bryony Snow, editor of top fashion magazine – Buttons and Bows. We need to impress Ms Snow – if she likes the show she is going to do a feature on it in the magazine, but most importantly we must put on a fabulous event for everyone in the village who has helped us to raise so much money for the hall."

All the girls in the class interrupted Miss Mallow with a huge cheer – Buttons and Bows was their favourite magazine, even though it was for grown-ups.

"But what is the show?" called out Tom impatiently.

"Well," continued Miss Mallow, "I'm going to write it myself but the words and songs will be based on a well-known story. You all know lots of stories so I thought it might be fun if you helped me to choose. You tell me your ideas and I'll write them on the board. Poppy's lovely storybook might give you some inspiration."

Every single child started calling out their favourites before Miss Mallow had even finished speaking – she could hardly keep up with them!

"Snow White and the Seven Dwarfs," called out one girl.

"Annie!" yelled another.

"Sleeping Beauty," suggested Lola, peering over to look in Poppy's book.

"Treasure Island!" shouted Charlie, to a loud cheer from the other boys.

"Little Red Riding Hood," said Helena.

"Cinderella!" cried Poppy, looking wistfully at the exquisite pictures in Great-Great-Granny Mellow's fairytale book.

"Yeah, Cinderella!" agreed several other girls.

"We love Cinderella."

"Peter Pan!" yelled Ollie.

"Enough!" gasped Miss Mallow. "My wrist is quite numb. We've got plenty to choose from now. I suggest you all copy down this list and have a good think about it overnight. Then tomorrow we can put it to a vote. The story with the most votes is the show that we will do."

Snow White & the Seven Dwarfs
Annie
Sleeping Beauty
Treasure Island
Little Red Riding Hood
Cinderella
Peter Pan

At break, Poppy, Honey, Sweetpea, Mimosa and Abi formed a huddle in the playground – they were desperate to talk about the show.

"Which story are you going to vote for?" asked Poppy.

"Cinderella!" replied the other four girls in unison – each imagining themselves in a starring role and dressed as a fairytale princess.

Poppy is taking part in a Pony Club competition with her cousin Daisy. They've both been practising like mad and they absolutely can't wait. But before long a whole series of things start to go wrong and it looks like Poppy might not be able to compete after all.

Will the Pony Club let Poppy enter the competition? Will Twinkletoes be well enough to jump and, most importantly, will Poppy ever get to be a Pony Club Princess? Find out in this brilliant new adventure.

MORE PRINCESS POPPY ADVENTURES
★ Pop Star Princess ★ Ballet Dreams ★
★ The Haunted Holiday ★ Fairytale Princess ★

Illustrated by Samantha Chaffey

ISBN 978-0-552-56655-1

£4.99
Can $8.95

7+

www.kidsatrandomhouse.co.uk
www.princesspoppy.com